PICKING UP SPEED

SUPER HUMAN

PICKING UP SPEED

RAELYN DRAKE

darby creek

MINNEAPOLIS

Darby Creek
A division of Lerner Publishing Group, Inc.
241 First Avenue North
Minneapolis, MN 55401 USA

For reading levels and more information, look up this title at
www.lernerbooks.com.

The images in this book are used with the permission of: iStock.com/Vladimirovic; iStock.com/aarrows; iStock.com/filadendron; MrVander/Shutterstock.com; iStock.com/sinemaslow.

Main body text set in Janson Text LT Std 12/17.5.
Typeface provided by Adobe Systems.

Library of Congress Cataloging-in-Publication Data

Names: Drake, Raelyn, author.
Title: Picking up speed / Raelyn Drake.
Description: Minneapolis : Darby Creek, [2018] | Series: Superhuman | Summary: "Natalie is shocked when she can suddenly run faster than humanly possible. As she moves up in the school track team, Natalie's new cocky attitude takes a toll on her relationships. She must decide if the super speed is worth it"— Provided by publisher.
Identifiers: LCCN 2017018574 (print) | LCCN 2017036378 (ebook) | ISBN 9781512498356 (eb pdf) | ISBN 9781512498318 (lb : alk. paper) | ISBN 9781541510500 (pb : alk. paper)
Subjects: | CYAC: Speed—Fiction. | Ability—Fiction. | Sisters—Fiction. | Conduct of life—Fiction. | Schools--Fiction. | High schools—Fiction. | Orphans—Fiction.
Classification: LCC PZ7.1.D74 (ebook) | LCC PZ7.1.D74 Pic 2018 (print) | DDC [Fic]—dc23

LC record available at https://lccn.loc.gov/2017018574

Manufactured in the United States of America
1-43582-33363-8/1/2017

To my friend, Kayla, and
her daughter, Natalie

SIXTEEN YEARS AGO, ON APRIL 12, SIX PEOPLE FROM AROUND THE COUNTRY WERE BORN WITH A HIDDEN SPECIAL ABILITY.

On their sixteenth birthday, they each develop their special ability for the first time. Whether they can soar through the clouds, run faster than the speed of light, or tear through a brick wall, all the teenagers must choose how to use their powers. Will they keep their abilities secret? Will they use them only to benefit themselves? Or will they attempt to help others—even if the risks are greater than they could imagine? One way or another, each teen will have to learn what it means to be . . . superhuman.

1

The morning of Natalie Santos's sixteenth birthday felt a whole lot like the morning before, when she was still fifteen. She had to admit, she had been hoping that turning sixteen would give her some sort of special insight into her life. Instead she just wished she could have gotten another three hours of sleep. Same as all the other mornings.

Natalie sighed and sat on the side of her bed, unwrapping a protein bar from the box in her nightstand. Rain pattered against the windows. April 12 looked more like February 12. *Isn't it supposed to be spring by now?* she thought.

She stared at the calendar on her wall, munching on the bar of chocolatey sawdust. There were green *x*'s on the days she did an extra workout, and she wasn't about to let herself slack off just because it was her birthday. She avoided looking at the calendar, with the red circle drawn around the following Saturday. The next track meet.

Just focus on making each practice count, she reminded herself as anxiety prickled in her stomach. *One day at a time.* She pulled her wavy, dark hair back into a ponytail. The sooner she got out of the house, the less time she would have to second-guess her motivation, and the less time she would have to convince herself to stay in bed and get an extra hour of sleep.

She quickly changed into her running clothes, laced up her new running shoes—an early birthday present from her sister, Maia—and headed out for her morning run. Mornings before school were the only time that Natalie could fit in these occasional extra runs, and her sister and grandparents would still be asleep.

Their parents had died in a car accident seven years ago, and the girls had lived with their grandparents ever since.

She set off down the quiet street, jogging to warm up. The rain was cold but not as heavy as it had looked from under her blankets.

Her new running shoes were still a little stiff, but they cushioned her feet and gave an extra spring to her stride compared to her old worn-down shoes. She focused on her running form, paying attention to her breaths and making sure not to smack her feet too hard on the ground.

Natalie was warmed up by the time she reached the park where she liked to practice sprints, but she wasn't sweating. That was unusual. Natalie had always sweated more than other people. Maia said that it was healthy, but when her sister sweated it looked more like a radiant glow of health. Natalie just tended to drip.

She did some quick stretches—lunging, jumping, and twisting—to loosen up her muscles and improve her range of motion.

The park's trail was paved with the same sort of rubberized material as the high school's track. It was much easier to run on than cement.

Natalie lowered herself into the starting sprint position, a kind of crouch with her fingertips touching the ground, one foot ahead of the other.

She spent a couple of minutes practicing the most important part of a sprint—the start. She worked on moving from her crouch to a sprint as quickly and smoothly as she could, being careful to come up gradually instead of standing up right away. She would let her momentum carry her for a few steps, then go right back into the starting position.

After she had done enough reps, Natalie launched herself into her first proper sprint of the morning. She headed down a trail that branched off the main path then looped back to rejoin it. She had measured the distance and knew that it was almost exactly 400 meters. Plus, the loop allowed her to practice running along curves.

Marathon runners had to learn how to pace themselves over long distances, but as a sprinter, Natalie knew the most important things were quick starts and intense bursts of speed. The 400-meter dash was the longest sprinting event, but it was still only one lap around the track. Natalie liked it because even if her start was a little off, she still might have a chance to narrow the gap before the end. Not that she was ever able to do that, but at least it was possible in theory.

Natalie was always one of the last in her heats to finish, and she consistently had one of the slowest times on the team for the 400. That was why she sometimes went out for these morning runs before school in addition to normal track practice after school with Maia and the rest of the team. The rows of *x*'s on her calendar proved that she had been doing some sort of training, rain or snow or shine, ever since the start of her sophomore year when Coach Yeung had agreed to let her try competing in running events. Her solo runs weren't as frequent now that she had track practices every week, but she still felt good that she was doing some kind of training nearly every day. She had spent her freshman year doing field events like shot put. Shot put was fine and Natalie was decent at it, but what she really loved was running.

Natalie sped down the path toward the tree, the wind whooshing in her ears.

And then, suddenly, she realized that she was no longer running on the loop. She was already back on the main path.

But she *couldn't* have just run 400 meters. It had only been a couple of seconds. It wasn't possible.

Natalie didn't always time her sprints in her before-school runs, but she had a pretty good idea of what a good sprint or a slow sprint felt like, and not nearly enough time had passed.

She slowed to a stop and turned around. The sign that marked the start of the loop trail was barely visible behind her. She was so far down the main path that she was near the paddleboat rental place along the river.

And even stranger, she wasn't out of breath.

A solid sprint usually left her panting.

Natalie shook her head and decided to sprint back the way she had come.

Again, she felt like she had barely reached her top speed before she made it back to the signpost.

What's going on? she wondered.

Natalie checked her watch and groaned. She had hit the snooze before getting out of bed this morning, which meant that if she wanted to get to school on time, she would have to cut her running practice short.

It usually took a full ten minutes to jog back to her house at a comfortable pace.

As Natalie ran, the wind whistled in her ears and the trees and houses sped past faster and faster until they blurred together with the morning fog. Part of her was aware that she was going incredibly fast, but the other part was more focused on wanting breakfast and coffee. She figured her senses must be lying to her. It was impossible to run so fast.

One minute and forty seconds later, she skidded to a stop in front of her house. Even

Maia couldn't run that far in under two minutes. Natalie examined her watch. It didn't seem to be broken, and the skeptical part of her brain was finding it harder to ignore this new evidence.

She pressed two fingers to her neck to feel her pulse. It was slightly quicker than usual, but usually at the end of her workouts it was pounding. Natalie frowned and went inside to shower and change for school, still convinced she was just imagining things this morning.

By the time Natalie got out of the shower, she was cutting it close to getting to school on time. She hurried downstairs and into the kitchen, dressed for school but with the towel wrapped around her wet hair.

"Morning, Abuela," she said, giving her grandma a peck on the cheek.

"There's the birthday girl! I made you breakfast."

Natalie looked down at the post-workout smoothie she had grabbed from the fridge. It was actually pretty tasty, but blueberries and kale mixed with protein powder didn't sound nearly as appetizing as scrambled eggs. And it was her birthday after all. She grabbed a plate but ignored the box of breakfast pastries on the counter. There would be birthday cake tonight anyway.

Maia walked into the kitchen, stifling a yawn as she poured herself coffee. "You better eat that quickly, Nat, or you're going to miss getting a ride to school with me."

"Aren't you gonna have breakfast?" Natalie asked between mouthfuls as she ate quickly.

Maia looked at the travel mug of coffee in her hand, shrugged, and grabbed a sweet roll from the counter.

Natalie's grandma sipped on a glass of orange juice. "Now, I've got a deadline coming up," she started. Their grandma wrote freelance articles for the local newspaper. "And your grandfather is volunteering at the shelter this afternoon, but we'll be celebrating your birthday tonight as soon as you two get home from track practice."

"It's track *and field*, Abuela," Maia corrected absently as she checked her newsfeed on her phone. "Don't forget the field part."

Natalie felt her face grow hot. "I don't even do shot put any more, Maia. We *both* do track now."

"You were really good at shot put, though—" Maia looked up from her phone, eyes wide, and added quickly, "Not that you're not good at running!"

Natalie ignored the comment and carried her dishes over to the sink. She grabbed her backpack, thinking back to her morning run.

Maybe all of her hard work *was* paying off. Maybe the early morning practice and endless training and kale smoothies were finally making a difference.

It's about time, she thought.

2

By the time Natalie got to track practice after school, her confidence from that morning was starting to wear off. It had been a long, tiring day, filled with pop quizzes and unusually boring lectures, and she was beginning to doubt what had happened.

I just imagined running that fast, she told herself. *There's no way I improved that much overnight.*

On Monday morning, she had struggled to shave even a half second off her time for the 400. Besides being her birthday, what made this dreary Tuesday any different? She had been working hard for months without much progress. It was doubtful it would suddenly start working now.

Dressed in her shorts and an old track team T-shirt, Natalie wandered over to where her friend, Jordan, was stretching and warming up on the turf in the center of the track.

"What did you think of the kale smoothie recipe?" Jordan asked.

"Surprisingly tasty," Natalie lied, thinking wistfully of the eggs she'd had for breakfast. She bent over to stretch her hamstrings.

"I know, right?" Jordan panted between jumping jacks. "But I might double the blueberries in proportion to the kale next time. It's hard to get the protein-carb-fiber balance right."

Natalie crossed one leg over the other and reached down to touch her toes. "Oh, of course," she deadpanned. "If my kale ratio is out of whack, I feel awful all day."

She nearly lost her balance as Jordan shoved her playfully. "Oh c'mon, before we started taking the nutrition and training stuff seriously, we were the slowest runners on the team."

Natalie rolled her eyes. "Jordan, I hate to break it to you, but we're *still* the slowest runners on the team."

Jordan made a pouting face. "Yeah, but we're faster than we used to be! And don't you feel healthier?"

"Don't get me wrong, I love the excuse to eat more fresh avocado and pineapple and stuff, but I could really do without adding kale and chia seeds to everything."

Jordan gasped in mock horror. "How dare you insult my beloved chia seeds!"

Coach Yeung called everyone over to the bleachers. Natalie looked over to where Maia was chatting with her friends from the varsity team. They were mostly seniors like her sister, but a lot of juniors and several sophomores also competed at the varsity level. Natalie was happy she could compete at all.

"All right, everyone, we've got the district meet coming up next weekend. Now remember, your main opponent is yourself. If you can beat your own personal bests, that's a win right there."

Jordan snorted quietly and Natalie had a hard time keeping a straight face.

With that, the coach clapped her hands and everyone broke into small groups to practice. After warming up, Jordan headed for the far corner of the field, where there was a straight strip of track designed specifically for practicing starts and short-distance sprints. Natalie turned to follow her when Coach Yeung called her over.

Natalie jogged over. "Yeah, Coach?" She took the opportunity to grab her water bottle from the bleachers.

"I just wanted to see how you were doing, Santos. Are you ready for the district meet next weekend?"

"Yep!" Natalie lied, gulping some water to hide her anxiety.

"Because I just wanted to let you know that it's not too late to switch events," Coach Yeung said. "You could still participate in a field event. I know you haven't done shot put since last year, but I'm sure it will come back to you pretty quickly."

Natalie liked Coach Yeung in general, but right now she had to restrain herself from squeezing her water bottle too tightly. She glanced toward the section of the field where the shot put girls were practicing their throwing technique before answering. "Are you saying you don't want me to run?"

"I know you've been working very hard all year," Coach Yeung said, "but your sprint times aren't quite . . . competitive, and I just wanted to make sure that you were choosing sprints because *you* wanted to, and not just because you felt like you had to."

Coach Yeung kept her eyes on Natalie's face, but Natalie could tell she was resisting the urge to look at Maia when she spoke. Maia currently held the school record for the fastest sprint time.

"I love running," Natalie said quietly, trying to ignore the queasy feeling in her stomach. "More than anything."

Coach Yeung smiled and clapped Natalie on her back. "Then you keep up the hard work, and don't let anyone tell you otherwise, okay, Santos? We all believe in you."

Natalie felt a blush creep into her cheeks as she went to join Jordan on the other side of the field where an assistant coach was helping the JV team practice sprints. She kept her head down as she hurried past the pole vaulting mats and the practice hurdles. Somehow the forced encouragement made her feel worse than any outright criticism would.

"What was that about?" Jordan asked as Natalie joined her. She looked at Natalie's face and rolled her eyes. "I know that face. Don't let it get you down. Coach is always trying to get me to"—she made air quotes—"'reconsider where my strengths lie.' I may come in close to dead last, but hey, if we're having fun then it doesn't matter, right?"

Natalie thought of her sister's bulletin board that was full of gold medals, not to mention the varsity patch on her letterman jacket. Natalie had a single bronze medal from a local shot put competition and a handful of participation ribbons.

"*Pfft*, yeah, who cares about winning?" She hoped she sounded more sincere than she felt.

"Cool kicks, by the way," Jordan said, pointing to Natalie's vibrant green running shoes. "Are they new?"

She nodded. "Birthday present from Maia."

"Aww, that was sweet of her," Jordan said. She looked over to where Maia and the rest of the varsity sprinters were doing practice heats on the main track. "Ugh, look at them! Who am I kidding? We're never going to be that fast." Jordan swept a hand up to her forehead in mock despair.

Natalie laughed, but she tried to ignore the twinge of jealousy she felt as she watched her sister run with an effortless grace and fluid motion that made sprinting look like the easiest thing in the world. "You just got done saying that having fun was more important than winning," she pointed out.

Jordan smirked. "I bet I'd have *lots* of fun if I was winning." She walked up to the starting blocks in the next heat. "Let's see if we can at least beat our personal bests."

Natalie certainly wasn't going to give up now. The season was almost over, and she had stuck it out so far. Quitting would be far more embarrassing than continuing to run slowly.

She got into the starting position, resting her feet against the starting blocks. She took a deep breath, and when the assistant coach said go, she took off with the other runners.

Natalie had wondered if her surprising speed that morning had been some sort of fluke. But as she ran she felt the familiar thrill of speed as her legs and arms pumped to build momentum. When she crossed the painted 200-meter mark, she felt like she was flying. She slowed to a stop and walked back to the coach with Jordan.

"How'd I do?" Natalie asked.

The coach's brow furrowed. "You improved on your personal best by ten seconds, Natalie."

"Cool!" she said.

"Cool?" Jordan repeated, panting. "That's all you have to say? This whole season, your biggest time improvement has been *one* second. And now you jump ahead by ten whole seconds?!"

Natalie shrugged and couldn't help but

grin. She was too thrilled by her progress to let it bug her.

"What's your secret?" Jordan asked, narrowing her eyes suspiciously.

"Umm, tons of water and protein?"

Jordan folded her arms. "If you say so. But I've got my eye on you, Santos," she said. She tried to keep a straight face but started laughing. Natalie laughed too.

She didn't say anything about Jordan ending up being one second *slower* than the week before.

3

Saturday morning, Natalie met Jordan at the track behind the middle school. It wasn't as nice as the track at the high school, but the asphalt surface was still more forgiving to run on than concrete sidewalks somewhere else. Plus, the middle school was across town and it was less likely they would run into someone they knew. It was bad enough having everyone watch their slow runs at practice.

After they'd spent the morning doing a series of lunges and jump squats and other bodyweight workouts followed by a one-mile jog, Jordan pulled her phone out of her bag. "I almost forgot," she said. "I found the coolest app. It's a super accurate speedometer that uses your phone's GPS. Then it maps out your route and tells you your time and average speed. And it records and logs each sprint so you can track your progress. Wanna try it out?"

Natalie grimaced. "Are you kidding? I'm *way* too tired to run a four hundred right now."

"Just do a one hundred or two hundred then," Jordan pleaded. "I just want to test it out."

"Fine," Natalie said, taking the phone from Jordan and sticking it in her shorts pocket. She sprinted down the straight part of the track. She had been exhausted, but all at once she got her second wind. She didn't feel like stopping after 100 meters, or even after 200 meters, so she ran a full lap around the track, slowing to a stop when she got back to Jordan.

Jordan stared at her for a second.

"So . . . are you going to go or not?" she asked, raising an eyebrow.

"What do you mean?" Natalie asked. "I just did it."

Jordan looked puzzled. "Did what?"

"My sprint."

Jordan snorted. "You did not! You've been standing her the whole time. Are you saying I blinked and I missed you running the fastest one hundred in the history of the sport?"

"Four hundred," Natalie mumbled, scuffing her shoe on the asphalt. "Do you want me to go again?"

Jordan took her phone from Natalie to check the speed. She frowned. "What . . ."

"What does it say?" Natalie tried to see the screen. She knew that was a fast sprint, but she wanted to know *how* fast.

The app was glitching—it kept blinking and freezing, but one number blinked over and over again. Natalie felt her heart skip a beat. The readout was saying 220 mph.

"That . . . that *can't* be right," Jordan murmured.

"*Two hundred twenty* miles per hour?" Natalie exclaimed. "But that's like the top speed for a race car or—" She paused to pull up the search function on her phone.

"That's like eight times faster than Usain Bolt," Jordan said. "And people are pretty sure he's the fastest man alive—"

"Get some perspective, Jordan!" Natalie held up her phone. "Forget the fastest *human*— it says here that the peregrine falcon can dive at speeds of over two hundred miles per hour, and it's the fastest member of the entire animal kingdom."

Jordan was still staring at the speedometer app in disbelief. "Maybe it's broken." She held her phone up to her ear and shook it.

"I don't know, I mean I *have* been drinking lots of water lately and focusing on getting enough protein for building muscle, you know . . ." Natalie trailed off as Jordan side-eyed her.

Natalie held up her hands. "I don't know what's going on any more than you do. Why don't you go next to prove the app isn't malfunctioning?"

Jordan sprinted 200 meters, then walked back slowly, looking exhausted from pushing herself at the end of what had already been a tough workout.

Natalie checked the app. Jordan's speed was barely out of the single digits. No blinking or freezing this time.

Jordan had Natalie go once more, just to make sure her first speed result hadn't been an error. This time, for the first time ever since she had started running, Natalie focused on slowing down as she ran. It was like running down an incredibly steep hill without picking up speed. It took all her effort to run slow when every instinct and all of her training told her to run as fast as she could.

When she got back to Jordan and showed her the phone, her friend's mouth dropped open. The speedometer app showed 49 mph.

Natalie's heart pounded with excitement. The smaller number was easier to get her head around, making it somehow more shocking than the impossibly large number. Natalie did the math on her phone's calculator: 49 miles per hour was 22 meters per second. "So even if I held back, at that speed I could finish the four hundred in—"

"Under twenty seconds," Jordan finished faintly. "That's not humanly possible."

Natalie shrugged. "Apparently it is?"

Jordan opened and closed her mouth a few times, as though her brain was still trying to process this information. "I'm pretty sure the world record is, like, forty-five seconds," she protested.

"Are you still trying to claim the speedometer is broken?"

"I wish I could," Jordan said. "But this time I saw you run the whole way." She ran a hand through her curls. "You were going so fast you were practically a blur. What's going on, Nat?"

"I honestly don't know," Natalie said. "Last week, I was my regular slowpoke self, and then Tuesday morning I ran from the park to my house in under two minutes. Your guess is as good as mine."

"Steroids?" Jordan said.

"*What?* No, of course I'm not taking steroids . . . Wait, are you actually trying to guess? It was a rhetorical question."

"Bionic legs?"

Natalie snorted. "I wish! Robot legs would be sweet. But still, no."

Jordan's eyes grew wide and she covered her mouth with her hand as she gasped.

"Whoa, wait. Didn't you say those shoes were a birthday present?" She pointed at Natalie's bright green shoes.

"I mean, yeah, my crazy new speed only started on my birthday, which was the first morning I wore these shoes . . ."

Jordan bounced on the balls of her feet, barely able to contain her excitement. "What if they're *magic* shoes?" she asked in an awed whisper.

Natalie wanted to laugh at the idea, but she and Jordan had been reading fantasy novels since they were kids. *What if?*

"Well, the only way to find out would be to switch shoes," Natalie said reluctantly, not wanting to give up her shoes if they really were the key to unlocking her newfound powers.

But they had to know for sure. She took off her shoes and switched with Jordan.

"Here," Natalie said as they laced up the shoes, "Let's race to the end of the track and back."

Natalie had reached the end of the track and blew past Jordan on her way back before Jordan had gone more than a couple of steps.

Jordan's face fell when Natalie tapped her on the shoulder and she realized what had happened. "Okay, so it's not the shoes."

"I guess not," Natalie said as they switched back.

Jordan alternated between staring at Natalie and staring at the track, muttering under her breath the whole time like she did when she was trying to work her way through a tough math problem.

Natalie hardly dared to believe it herself. She *wouldn't* believe it if she hadn't seen the surface of the track flash by so quickly that the painted lane lines blended into one, if she hadn't felt the wind whipping by her ears so fast it thumped against her ear drums.

"So, what then?" Jordan asked. "How did you get it?"

Natalie could see that the dazed expression in her eyes had been replaced by sharp curiosity. Her friend liked making plans and finding solutions, and Natalie could tell Jordan had reasoned out some sort of answer. *Now if only she'd tell me what it is*, Natalie thought.

"Huh?" she asked Jordan, still feeling lost and a little frustrated. "How did I get what?"

Jordan smiled like she thought it should be obvious. "Your superpower. How did you get the power of super speed?"

Natalie blinked in surprise, trying to figure out how her friend had reached such an eccentric conclusion. Not that superpowers were any more improbable than magic shoes . . .

Natalie shook her head slowly. "I'm not sure. I guess I just woke up like this. It's not like superpowers run in my family."

"Last time I checked, your grandparents were pretty normal."

"And I didn't notice any cousins wearing capes and tights at my fifteenth last year."

Natalie's mind was still spinning. She needed a moment to think this all over. She cleared her throat. "That totally reminds me, have you figured out what you want to do for your sweet sixteen party next month? We should probably start planning now—"

"Don't try to change the subject, Nat!"

Jordan said, hands on her hips. "What we need to plan is how you're going to keep all of this a secret."

"Why does it need to be a secret?" Natalie asked.

Jordan scoffed. "Why do you think superheroes need secret identities?"

"But I don't want to be a superhero!" Natalie protested. "I don't have that sort of savior complex."

Jordan laughed. "Still, now that you're some sort of superhuman, we should start training you to run a little more slowly. Coach will notice something is weird if you start running at the speed of light."

Natalie opened her mouth to correct her friend, but Jordan frowned and held up a hand to silence her while she pulled out her phone to do a quick search. "Okay, fine, that would be like six hundred seventy million miles per hour, so not quite that fast. But you get the idea."

"Speed of sound?" Natalie suggested.

"You're still a ways off, but let me know if you find you can suddenly outrun a jet fighter."

Natalie chuckled. "I think Coach would definitely notice if there was a sonic boom every time I ran."

"Okay," Jordan said, "let's jog back to my place and we can stretch while we watch a movie. *Last* one home wins."

As soon as she started running, Natalie knew that she was going to "lose" by beating Jordan home. It was too hard to focus on controlling her speed when every footfall, every breath sent a single word pounding through her mind like a drumbeat.

An impossible word that sparked through her like electricity.

Superhuman.

4

Late the next afternoon, Natalie rode her bike to a nearby nature trail. It was technically a rest day, according to her training program, but Natalie was sore from strength training the day before, so she decided she would just go for a slow jog to loosen up her stiff muscles. Besides, it was good to go for endurance runs occasionally to prepare for the last 100 meters of the 400.

She started at an easy pace, her feet crunching on the woodchips of the looping path through the woods. Natalie had always loved running, but it tended to be hard work. Over the last few days, though, it felt like the easiest thing in the world. Before she even realized it, her slow jog had turned into a pace that matched the fastest sprinters on her team, including her sister. And even then, it was still an easy pace for her.

Natalie continued at that pace, enjoying the feeling of blood pumping through her veins. She realized she had already passed the turn where she'd usually loop back, but it felt too good to stop as the adrenaline surged through her. The world around her flashed by in a haze of green leaves and golden afternoon sunlight.

She had nearly finished the full five-mile trail when the dizziness hit her out of nowhere. Fatigue washed over her, and her leg muscles felt like jelly. She stumbled, and her momentum sent her flying. She rolled to a stop in the grass on the side of the trail. She blinked, dazed, at the bright blue sky through the leaves of the trees then slowly sat up, groaning. She felt like she had run a marathon instead of five miles.

Her head was pounding and her throat was so dry she could hardly swallow. Natalie unclipped her water bottle and chugged it all. She staggered to her feet and leaned against a tree for balance, her legs shaking. She grimaced at the stabbing pain of a stitch in her side. Straightening up, Natalie clasped her hands together and rested them on top of her head with her elbows out to the side. She stood like that until the cramp in her rib cage had loosened and she could breathe more easily.

She brushed the woodchips off her knees and elbows and winced when she realized the woodchips had left stinging scratches smeared with blood and dirt.

Natalie nearly gasped when she finally turned her attention to her shoes. Her brand-new shoes were tattered and full of holes. It looked like she had owned them for two years instead of less than a week. How had she not noticed? Had today's run really been enough to finish them off?

She hobbled back to where she'd left her bike and started to pedal home, her bike weaving in tired zigzags along the sidewalk. All she wanted to do was collapse in bed and sleep, but she slowed down when she passed the local running store. She scrunched her eyes shut and heaved a sigh. There was no way around it, she realized. Maia would freak out if she saw the state of the birthday present she had given Natalie only a few days ago.

Natalie leaned her bike against the street lamp. She was honestly too exhausted to even care about using the bike lock. She shuffled wearily into the store.

The clerk behind the counter looked up as the electronic shop bell chimed. His eyes widened as he took in the extent of her blood and dirt stains. "You . . . ah, looking for anything in particular that I can help you with?"

Natalie felt another wave of dizziness wash over her as she shook her head, and she tried to focus on not passing out. She pointed at her shoes. "Need another pair of these," she mumbled.

"No kidding," the clerk said with a hint of nervous laughter. "What, did you send those through the dryer?" He went over to the shelves of shoeboxes lining the store, asked her size, and grabbed a box. As she waited, Natalie eyed a display case of energy gel packs.

"You sure you want the exact same pair?" he asked. "We just got some great new—"

"I'm sure," Natalie grunted. She grabbed a handful of the gel packs. "I'll take some of these too."

The clerk raised an eyebrow but rang up her purchase without making another comment.

Natalie muttered thanks and went to sit on the bench outside the shop to lace up her new shoes. Her sister had gone all out for her birthday; Natalie had managed to ruin what was apparently a very expensive set of running shoes.

She sighed grumpily, wishing she hadn't had to use the cash that her grandparents had given her for her birthday—it was supposed to be for fun things like makeup and movie tickets.

She tore open and eagerly ate one of the energy gels. Feeling a little better as the carbs fixed her blood sugar, she dumped her ruined shoes in the trash can and headed home. After a hot bath, an early dinner of an entire bag of chicken nuggets, and several glasses of water, Natalie collapsed into bed while the sun was still up. She slept in and missed her Monday morning run for the first time in months.

5

At Monday's practice, Natalie could hardly wait to show off her new speed. She felt much better after a full night's sleep and several large meals. On reflection, it seemed obvious that her body wasn't capable of maintaining super speed over long distances without refueling. She would have to be careful not to run at her top speed for too long, as well as make sure she took in enough calories to maintain her intense energy levels. That certainly explained why she had been so hungry over the past week.

"Like I said," Jordan whispered when Natalie had told her about this, "you need to be careful how you use these powers."

Coach Yeung was giving a pep talk that involved motivational quotes about effort and grit, and then she shared the current best times in the school and in the district. Natalie was only half paying attention, but she heard Maia's name. Maia's name was *always* on the list.

Natalie felt like she was being scolded by Jordan, and it annoyed her. "I still don't understand what you're getting at."

"Well," Jordan started, fiddling with her hands, "even if you don't get drafted into some sort of top secret superhero society and start fighting dangerous supervillains, then at the very least you'll be kicked off the team for cheating."

Natalie hissed back, "How is it cheating?"

"Ladies," Coach Yeung warned, looking straight at Natalie and Jordan, "please pay attention. I was just about to announce that Maia Santos has once again set a school record. Let's hear it for Maia!"

As their teammates whooped and applauded, Jordan muttered, "To the surprise of absolutely no one."

"Watch it, that's my sister," Natalie said halfheartedly. She secretly agreed with Jordan, though. It was sometimes annoying to have such a perfect and talented sister. And everyone had taken notice that the fastest and slowest runners on the team shared a last name.

***

"Okay fine," Jordan said as they ran up the bleachers together during warm-ups. "Even if I know that you're not doing something to cheat, Coach won't know that. It'll look totally suspicious."

Jordan's right, Natalie thought. The school had very strict policies for competing in sports, and she doubted that Coach Yeung would believe her explanation of "I just woke up one morning with superpowers!"

"What if I just increase my times really gradually?" Natalie suggested.

Jordan nodded as they pounded back down the bleachers. "Yeah, no more than a couple of seconds faster."

"I won't be the fastest person on the team. But hey, as long as I'm not the slowest, right?" Natalie laughed.

"Yep," Jordan said. They had reached the bottom of the bleachers, and Jordan jogged off without saying another word to join a group of girls who were doing drills across the field.

Jordan's reply had seemed a little gruff, Natalie thought. It took her a second to realize why. If her own times improved, the slowest person on the team would be Jordan.

***

Natalie surprised everyone on the team, including herself, when Coach Yeung asked if anyone wanted to run a practice 400 and she was the first to volunteer.

"Great attitude," Coach Yeung told Natalie as she took her place behind the starting line alongside three JV girls.

"Runners to your marks!" Coach Yeung yelled, getting her stopwatch ready.

As Natalie got into the starting position, anxiety briefly seized her. *What am I doing?*

she thought. *I'm going to look like such an idiot when I come in dead last, like I always do.* Natalie thought she could hear the rest of the team murmuring, but that could have been her imagination. *They're probably taking bets on how badly I'll lose.* Natalie could feel her teeth grind at the thought.

"Set!"

Natalie lifted her torso into the ready position, pulling up her back knee. The anxiety cleared and was replaced by single-minded focus.

"Go!"

Natalie's start wasn't as smooth or quick as she would have liked, even with superpowers. She knew that she had stood up a little too quickly. But as soon as she hit her stride, Natalie could hardly keep from smiling. She was already in love with this newfound freedom. Usually she trained to try to get her body to go faster, and instead it seemed just as clumsy and sluggish as ever. Now, when she set her sights down the track, her body responded like a well-oiled machine. She felt graceful and strong like she never had before.

It took all of her concentration to reign herself in. She matched her pace to the girl who was currently in second place. She felt like she was running through molasses, even though the other runners were clearly trying their hardest. Natalie made a show of pumping her arms and legs even though she hardly needed to.

In the last 100 meters, as they rounded the second curve and headed down the straightaway for the finish line, Natalie did her best to avoid the ingrained habit to speed up for the final push. She let the other girl overtake her at the last moment and came in third.

It took her a moment to realize that the whoops and scattered applause of her teammates was meant for her.

"Wow!" Coach Yeung said. "Way to hustle, Santos! Someone's clearly been training."

Natalie beamed. Coach Yeung usually said things like "shake it off" or "excellent effort." This had to be the first time Coach

Yeung seemed to be genuinely impressed by her performance. Even better was the look of surprise on her sister's face. When she caught her sister's eye, Maia smiled and gave Natalie a thumbs-up, which Natalie returned.

Jordan gave Natalie a grim smile as she walked past to take her place in the next practice heat. Coach Yeung expected everyone to do it occasionally. Natalie and Jordan used to avoid them like the plague, only going when Coach Yeung absolutely forced them. Coach Yeung had called out Jordan at the beginning of today's practice, letting her know that she would be expected to participate today. And now Jordan walked toward the track with the slow step and bowed head of someone going to meet an executioner.

Natalie clapped and cheered loudly. "Go, Jordan! C'mon, girl! You got this!"

The runners sank into their starting positions, and when Coach Yeung said go they took off around the track. Well, "took off" was a loose term. Natalie used to watch her teammates race with a pang of envy for their easy strides and flawless form. Now they all seemed *so* slow that it was agonizing to watch.

And Jordan was the slowest of all.

Painfully slow, Natalie thought, especially when she realized that only a couple of weeks ago, that had been her. Jordan was fit, but some people were just slower runners. That didn't mean they couldn't get faster, they just had to work harder at it.

Natalie had thought that was true of herself too, although it seemed unfair that Maia would get all the athletic genes in the family and she wouldn't get any. But now that she had unlocked this superpower or whatever it was, she felt as though she had been meant to be fast all along. Her slowness had been a fluke, and now she had reached her true potential. It was an amazing feeling.

After a few more heats, Coach Yeung ended practice and everyone headed inside to shower and change.

As Natalie waited in the hallway outside the locker rooms, Kristin, one of Maia's varsity friends, motioned Natalie over. Natalie went over to join her sister and her friends.

"Your run was super impressive, Natalie," Kristin said.

"It really was," Maia chimed in. "Great work, Nat. That had to be, what, way better than your last personal best."

Natalie nodded but left out the exact numbers on how *much* better it was. "Yep, I've been doing a lot of extra training."

"Like what?" a senior named Jimmy asked her. Natalie recognized him from the boys' varsity track team.

"Oh you know, strength training, lots of protein. The usual."

"Awesome," Jimmy said.

"Hey," Kristin said, "we were planning to catch a movie after practice. You wanna join?"

"Yeah, you should come," Maia said. "I feel like we never get to hang out. Well, outside of practice at least."

Natalie was torn for a moment. She hadn't made any solid plans, but she and Jordan usually spent Monday evenings getting Thai takeout and binge-watching their favorite shows. But it wasn't like she had promised her friend. That was just what they usually did.

"Uh, sure, sounds great."

Maia, Kristin, and Jimmy started walking toward the doors to the parking lot where Maia had parked. Natalie had wanted to check in with Jordan first, but to be honest, she was worried that if she didn't stick close she would get left behind accidentally. Or they would decide that they had better things to do than to wait for a girl who wasn't even on junior varsity, even if she was the sister of one of the team captains.

Outside, she saw Jordan waiting by the bike rack. Natalie settled for a quick wave to get her attention, then pointed at Maia and her friends, then waggled her thumbs to mime "text me." Jordan smiled and waved back. Natalie hoped that meant that she was cool with it. She could apologize later if she needed to.

6

When Maia and Natalie got home after the movie that night, they found their grandpa sitting in the living room reading a book. They could hear the rapid clacking of computer keys from their grandma's study.

"Who said you could stay out so late on a school night?" he asked them, with a stern expression that wouldn't have fooled anyone. He chuckled and broke into a grin. "How was the movie?"

"Pretty good, Abuelo," Maia said. "But the really exciting news is that little Miss Natalie here beat her personal best in the four hundred today!" Maia grabbed Natalie by the shoulders and paraded her in front like she was some sort of champion poodle.

"Oh, hush," Natalie said, grinning in spite of herself. "It wasn't that great."

"Nonsense!" their grandpa said. "Beating a personal best is always something to celebrate." He stood up. "'This calls for some ice cream."

Natalie and Maia followed him into the kitchen, where he served them each a bowl of ice cream as they all sat at the table.

"Oh!" Natalie exclaimed. They both looked at her. "I almost forgot, but Maia is neglecting to mention the fact that she set the school record for the two hundred. Again."

"I wish they gave you kids report cards for track," their grandpa said. "I would plaster the fridge with them. I'd probably have enough by this point to repaper the guest bedroom."

"There's always ribbons and medals," Natalie reminded him. "And Maia has her letter."

"Speaking of, the next track meet is this weekend, right?" their grandpa asked, even though Natalie could read TRACK MEET in big letters on the calendar on the fridge from across the room.

"Yep," Maia said, swallowing a spoonful of ice cream. "I can't believe my last high school season's already almost halfway over. State will be here before we know it. I have to admit, I'm nervous. Ever since I got that scholarship, I've been worried it'll jinx me."

Natalie snorted. "Maia, you're the best runner in the school. Even if you fail miserably at the state competition, they're not going to take away your scholarship. Not even if you come in . . . second! Gasp! The horror!"

Maia elbowed her playfully as their grandpa laughed.

"And hey," Maia said, "you're going to have a real chance of qualifying for State and bringing home a medal in the four hundred if you run like you did today. Our school has the best runners, so if you can beat any of them, then you can definitely beat kids from other schools."

Natalie rolled her eyes. "There's no way I'll qualify for State."

But inside, she knew that she could now. She wasn't sure if it was wise to risk improving that much that quickly. But it had always been her dream to qualify for State. And now she had the opportunity.

***

Before bed, Natalie blended a berry and kale smoothie for the next day's breakfast. She took a picture of herself pretending to munch on an entire handful of raw kale and sent it to Jordan with a text that said, *Can't stop won't stop!!!*

Jordan texted back a laughing emoji.

Natalie was pretty sure that meant that Jordan had no hard feelings from getting ditched earlier. Natalie set her alarm for her morning run and went to sleep feeling better than she had in a long time.

***

The next couple of mornings before school, Natalie made sure to keep practicing going slowly enough to look believable. To look normal. After a while, she got the hang of going slowly enough to not raise any eyebrows or crush any records, but fast enough that she still enjoyed it. Compared to how fast she knew she was capable of going, it was kind of like power walking instead of sprinting, but if that's what it took, so be it.

Anything was better than the constant feeling of disappointment she used to feel from trying to increase her running speed and failing. Sure, she had improved her time little by little, month after month. But she found it hard to believe that beating your own personal bests was really all that fulfilling if you always came in last. Sometimes she had finished so far behind the others that they had time to stop running, turn around, and watch her cross the finish line. The seconds from when she saw the rest of them cross the finish line until when she huffed and puffed her way across seemed endless. Jordan was slow too, and that solidarity was the only thing that kept them going sometimes.

But the times that Natalie lost races were thankfully not the only part of track. She loved getting to hang out with Jordan after school. Improving her personal bests gave her goals to work toward. And besides, she and Maia had a lot more to talk about. Natalie loved her sister, but Maia was two years older and about to head off to college, where she hoped to study chemistry. Natalie was more interested in her history class than science, so track gave her something special to share with her sister.

And she enjoyed the running itself more than anything. Field events like shot put had been fun, but running—feeling the adrenaline course through her veins—that was what made her truly happy. So if she got to be good at something she loved, then so much the better.

It wasn't like anyone got hurt. Someone always had to lose; that was how competition worked.

And Natalie was done losing.

7

The district competition that weekend marked one of the first times that Natalie had looked forward to a track meet with eager anticipation instead of nerve-wracking dread. This would be her first chance to show that she had improved as a runner.

After waiting for hours—chatting with Jordan and grabbing one of the free hot dogs they served for lunch—*finally* it was time for the 400-meter dash.

Now Natalie followed closely on the heels of the sprinter in front of her. She had never realized how much fun races could be when she actually stood a chance of winning. She tried to hold herself back on the final stretch. She didn't need to be the fastest. She could just enjoy coming in second.

But then she heard the cheers of her teammates and their family members in the stands and realized that some of them were shouting her name. For the first time in her life, people were cheering for her and not Maia. It was time for the other Santos sister to take her place in the spotlight.

The thrill of it was too much, and Natalie found her speed picking up. She couldn't help it.

She wanted to go fast.

She needed to go fast.

She needed to be *the fastest*.

Adrenaline surging, Natalie pulled ahead and easily beat the runner in front. She crossed the finish line and raised her arms in victory, whooping excitedly along with the spectators. It was easy to beat the junior varsity runners. She only had to use a fraction of her new ability to be able to leave them in the dust.

Natalie grabbed her water bottle from a table near the finish line and downed the whole thing. She jogged over to where Jordan waited on the sidelines and held out her hands for a high five.

"That was amazing!" Jordan said, giving her a hug. She looked around to see if anyone was listening and then lowered her voice. "But I thought you had said you didn't want to draw too much attention to yourself?"

Natalie shrugged, grinning. "Why waste an opportunity like this?"

Jordan bit her lip. "I still think it's kind of unfair."

After the meet ended, Coach Yeung walked over and shook her hand, smiling proudly. "Can I just say, Santos, that your progress lately has just been inspiring? I've always said that anyone can improve their times with the right focus, nutrition, fitness, and hard work. Not everyone is built to be an Olympic sprinter like Usain Bolt, but everyone has potential to improve, no matter their skill level."

Natalie wondered where Coach Yeung was going with this. "Thanks, Coach. I've been working really hard lately." Well, technically the hard work didn't seem to have any direct effect on her new and marvelous abilities. But there was no denying that she had put in the time and effort and it was nice to get some recognition for all the mornings she had hauled herself out of bed before dawn.

"I wanted to let you know—if you keep up these times at our meets over the next few weeks, I think you'll be able to run for the varsity team in the regional competition. Then, depending on how you do, you could compete in the qualifying race for the state finals."

Somehow, even with the confidence of her newfound abilities, the thought of getting bumped up to varsity hadn't occurred to Natalie. Varsity was her sister's domain, a level of talent that Natalie thought would always be unattainable. And competing at State had always seemed like a dream rather than an actual opportunity.

"Really?" she asked, trying to keep the squeak of surprise out of her voice. "As a sophomore?"

"It's less common to have sophomores on the varsity team, sure, but when one shows the talent and grit that you have, it's an obvious choice to move them up."

Natalie noticed Jordan chatting with her grandparents and sister. She felt a stab of guilt as she thought about breaking the news to her friend. But varsity practiced with the rest of the team, so it wasn't like she was abandoning Jordan, not really. She told herself that if Jordan were in the same position, she would want Jordan to seize the opportunity. Natalie pushed aside her doubts and turned to Coach Yeung and smiled. "I'd be honored!"

"Good," said Coach Yeung. "I'd like to have you start running in some heats with varsity at practices so you can get used to their times. Stop by my office this week and we'll come up with a new practice schedule for you."

Just in time for Regionals, Natalie thought.

***

At home later that evening, as she sat down with her family around the kitchen table for dinner, Natalie was thrilled to be able to tell her grandparents the good news.

Maia explained, grinning excitedly. "Usually Coach Yeung would just wait until next year, but she wanted to make sure you were able to compete at the varsity level for a few meets this season. You still have to make it through the regional meet before you can qualify for State, but with the way you're running now, I don't think there will be any chance of you *not* qualifying." She gave Natalie a side hug. "You're going to be the Queen of the Four Hundred!"

"What does that make you?" Natalie asked.

"Duh, Grand Empress Supreme of the Two Hundred."

Natalie laughed along with her sister, but she felt a little awkward. She wasn't sure she would ever get used to people talking about her running performance this way. Usually people talked about track around with her with lots of "don't worry, you'll get 'em next time" before switching their attention to Maia, who always seemed to have at least three medals glittering around her neck. Hearing Maia talk about her this proudly and with this much admiration made Natalie blush.

"I can't believe both of our granddaughters are shaping up to be track stars!" their grandma exclaimed.

"Your parents would have been incredibly proud," their grandpa added, his eyes glistening ever so slightly. Maia squeezed his hand.

"Natalie," said their grandma, "would you be okay if I wrote about you in this article I'm doing on high school sports? I might just need a quote or two from you. And a picture of you from the district meet."

Natalie coughed in surprise. "Wouldn't you want to interview Maia for that? She placed first in her events."

"She's listed with the other winners, but I'd really like to have someone talk about what it's like to work hard to improve at a sport. Our Maia is just naturally talented, but you have been working so hard to improve. I know you slip out to go running before the sun is even up. That's dedication!"

Natalie felt uncomfortable being compared to her sister like this. "Maia practices a lot too . . ."

Maia chimed in. "No, don't be silly, Nat. Abuela is right, I tend to coast when I should be pushing myself. You've been giving it one hundred ten percent effort this year."

Well, if Maia is okay with it, Natalie thought. It did sound kind of cool to be quoted in an article. Her grandma mentioned Maia in her articles about the results of track meets plenty of times, but Natalie didn't think she had ever been mentioned before. There hadn't really been a reason for her to be mentioned.

8

The following week, Natalie stood in the hallway outside the school's weight room. There was no track practice on Fridays, but Natalie had been planning on meeting Jordan after class to work on strength training. Natalie had been so focused on her times over the past two weeks that they hadn't seen each other much at practice, so she was looking forward to hanging out together. The room was locked outside of school hours, but students on varsity teams received special keycards and Coach Yeung had loaned her one to help her prep for Regionals. Natalie had been looking forward to using the weight lifting machines and other specialized workout equipment. She thought Jordan had been excited too, but her friend was already half an hour late.

Natalie waited for a couple more minutes. Most of the fluorescent lights had been turned off, and the hallways of the school were dim and filled with eerie echoes. Natalie was a little creeped out that she was probably the only person in the building. Even the teachers and janitors left early on Fridays. *At least I could always outrun anyone who tried to chase me,* Natalie thought with a wry smile.

But she had been hoping that the lack of people would mean that she and Jordan would have the weight room to themselves and that they could talk in private about everything that had happened lately.

Bored, Natalie briefly considered seeing if she could run along walls like a ninja if she got going fast enough, but she didn't want to end up on the school security footage.

Finally, she sighed and texted Jordan.

You coming?

Several minutes later, Jordan replied: *Sorry, thought you had plans. Went home.*

There was no way that was true. Natalie had stopped by Jordan's locker that morning to confirm. Jordan had given her a tight smile, but Natalie had chalked it up to early morning tiredness and stress about the upcoming math quiz. Natalie wondered if Jordan was mad at her. It was so hard to tell over text.

While she was thinking this over, her phone buzzed again. Jordan had added:

Besides, not like you need extra training, right?!

Natalie frowned. She could tell when her friend was only pretending everything was fine. But it was clear that Jordan had bailed, and Natalie could sense the sarcasm in her friend's message.

Natalie knew that she hadn't been a very attentive friend lately, but she wondered what specifically had upset Jordan to the point that she didn't want to hang out. Not just that, but upset her to the point that she *lied* about not wanting to hang out. Was it because Natalie was no longer a slow runner? She and

Jordan had become closer out of solidarity as the slowest people on the track team, and a lot of their hangouts involved training to run faster or talking about training. But just because Natalie was fast now didn't mean that she didn't still want to hang out with Jordan. She'd always figured their friendship extended beyond the track team.

Surely Jordan couldn't be mad about the superpower thing. It wasn't like Natalie had planned on getting it. And even though she had only had her powers for a few weeks, they seemed so much a part of her—of her identity now—that it didn't make sense to hate them. Because hating her superpowers would be like hating *her.*

Natalie texted Jordan back, deciding to pretend like nothing was wrong.

No big deal! I'll see you this weekend.

Jordan didn't reply.

But a second later, Natalie got a text from Kristin asking if she wanted to hang out with the rest of that group at their usual coffee shop.

Natalie looked down at her workout clothes. She just had to change.

Sure, I'll be there in five.

Natalie sped toward home, not caring if anyone saw her.

***

When Natalie showed up at the coffee shop in what she hoped was a trendy outfit, Kristin and Jimmy waved her over to their table in the corner. Natalie grabbed a seat, smoothing her windblown hair.

She opened her mouth to speak when Maia came to the table, carefully balancing three drinks.

"Well, it took forever but here's our hot chocolate—" With the steaming hot beverages safely set down on the table, Maia looked up and stopped midsentence.

"Natalie?" Maia stared at her, then her eyes darted sideways toward Kristin, and Natalie thought she saw her sister's eyebrow twitch upward in an unspoken question.

"Hey," Natalie said. Why did Maia seem

surprised to see her?

Then she realized that Maia was carrying three hot cocoas, not four, and there were only three chairs at the table.

Face burning as she realized she had accidentally taken Maia's seat, Natalie jumped up to grab a chair from an empty table.

Kristin hurried to cover the awkward silence. "I texted her to see if she wanted to hang out," she told Maia. "You were in line for ages."

"I thought you were meeting Jordan to train after school?" Maia asked Natalie.

"Nah, she had test to study for, so we rescheduled," Natalie lied.

"Training on a Friday night?" Jimmy said. "That's some crazy dedication."

"No wonder you're crushing all the competition," Kristin said. "If I practiced a million hours a week, I would be super fast too." She laughed.

Natalie felt a little embarrassed. She wanted people to think of her as the talented one, not as the dork who trained on Friday nights.

She made a show of rolling her eyes. "Well, I usually wouldn't but I had promised Jordan I would help her improve her time."

Natalie immediately felt guilt twisting her stomach for throwing her friend under the bus like that.

Jimmy snorted. "Good luck with that. Some people just aren't meant to be runners."

Kristin elbowed him. "That's not nice," she laughed. "I'm sure she tries her hardest. It's always sad though when people like that work so hard and it just doesn't help. It kinda breaks your heart."

Maia scowled. "No one is naturally talented, Kristin. Even professional athletes have insane training programs."

"It helps to have good genes, though," Natalie said in a stage whisper, gesturing at herself and Maia.

Kristin and Jimmy laughed, but Natalie thought she saw her sister give her a look. Natalie wasn't sure why she was saying things like this. She supposed it was because she was still mad at Jordan. Even if Jordan seemed to think Natalie was the problem, that didn't mean that Natalie deserved the cold shoulder.

"Anyway," Natalie said, "could you believe that new drill Coach made us do at practice yesterday? It was brutal. I thought my legs would fall off." She chuckled at her own joke.

No one else seemed quite as interested in this conversation topic. "Yeah, it was pretty tough," Kristin said with a tight smile.

Natalie wished she had a drink so that she had something to do with her hands. "So which school's team do you think has the best chance at Regionals? I've heard Hamilton High could be pretty steep competition—"

Maia sighed dramatically and rolled her eyes. "Hey, it's Friday and the meet isn't until Sunday. Let's please talk about anything besides track. We already sell our souls to the team the rest of the week, let's enjoy our freedom for the moment."

Kristin and Jimmy laughed. Natalie joined in but felt like she'd reacted a second too late. They started talking about a band Natalie had never heard of that was going to be in town that summer for an eighteen and up concert that she wouldn't even be able to go to. She pretended to check her phone, just in case her blush was visible. Jordan still hadn't texted her back. But when Natalie thought back to some of things she had said about Jordan that evening, she wasn't sure she could really find her silence surprising. She desperately hoped that the comments she had made wouldn't get back to Jordan. If she thought Jordan was mad at her now . . .

As the others chatted and laughed and Natalie pretended to enjoy herself, she realized that she couldn't think of a single topic of conversation that didn't have something to do with track or running or fitness in general. It had literally been her main focus for most of the school year. And between training, thinking about and planning for training, and things like homework and sleep, she hadn't had time for much else.

She realized she didn't even know what sort of music her sister listened to, although apparently this band was one of her all-time favorites.

Ever since their parents had died, Natalie and Maia had stuck close to each other, facing the world as a team. And now Natalie had spent the past year being jealous of Maia or competing for attention with Maia or longing to be more like Maia. But all of that had to do with Maia's track performance, not with her as a person.

Natalie clenched her teeth. She could hang out with her sister and make up with Jordan *after* the state competition when the track season was over. Natalie was too committed to back out now. She was going to get the win she deserved.

9

Over the next few weeks, Natalie continued
to practice with the varsity girls. She ran in
JV races at meets and soon she was winning
every time.

By the time Regionals rolled around, her
new times were so consistent that she was
officially bumped up to the varsity team.
Natalie found it almost as easy to beat the
varsity athletes as it had been to beat the ones
on JV. It was a more delicate balance of keeping
her pace not too slow and not too fast. But
she had undeniably crushed the students from
other schools in the area. On the way home,
she had joked with Maia that with how far

behind the next fastest runner finished, they should have just given her the first, second, *and* third place medals. Maia had seemed less amused by this than Natalie had been.

Of course what really mattered was that she, Natalie Nicole Santos, would get to compete at Sectionals, the qualifying race for the state finals. She could actually go to *State*.

***

The next week at school, Natalie stopped by Coach Yeung's office during her free period.

The door was open, and Coach Yeung looked up when Natalie rapped on the doorframe to announce her presence.

"Hey, Santos," she said. "What's up?"

Natalie didn't see any reason to beat around the bush. "I have a question about Sectionals. Would it be possible to try to qualify in more sprint events than just the four hundred?"

"*Just* the four hundred?" Coach Yeung repeated, smirking. "The four hundred is one of the harder sprints to master, you know."

"Honestly, I could use more of a challenge."

"When you spend so much time training for a particular event, it can be hard to just jump into a new event without properly training for it. The four hundred requires a different set of skills than the other sprints."

"I'm pretty sure I can win them," Natalie said.

She had tried to keep the scoff out of her voice, but Coach Yeung still stared at her for a moment before speaking. "Fine, I don't think it's too late to get you signed up for the two hundred."

"Thank you so much!" Natalie turned to leave. "I really appreciate it—"

"Santos?"

Natalie paused. "Yeah?"

"I just wanted to give you some friendly advice. I know that somehow, recently, you've become very good at sprinting. You've gone from being one of the slowest people on the team to one of the fastest."

Natalie didn't say anything. She wondered where Coach Yeung was going with this. Did she know about her superpowers? Or worse, did she suspect her of cheating?

Coach Yeung continued. "Such a rapid improvement can be exciting, I get that. But you need to keep in mind that sometimes the slow, hardworking runner is a better asset to the team than the fast runner who doesn't have to work for it."

She smiled at Natalie. "I'm not trying to scold you, so stop looking at me like that. I'm just saying that you shouldn't forget the tremendous effort and unfailing positive attitude that got you this far."

Natalie's head was buzzing. "Um, thanks, Coach."

"Good luck at Sectionals, Santos."

***

On Tuesday after they got home from practice, Maia approached Natalie in the kitchen. "Can we talk?"

Natalie pretended not to notice her sister's foul mood. "Sure," she said, flashing an innocent smile.

"In private," Maia clarified. She shot a meaningful look at their grandma, who seemed to be pretending not to notice any tension between the sisters. Natalie dropped the teasing act and followed her sister up to her bedroom, heart rate quickening as she tried to figure out why her sister seemed so mad at her. Annoyed she could understand. But angry?

Natalie joined her sister in her bedroom and shut the door behind her. "What's up?" she asked, dreading the answer.

Maia put a hand to her forehead and closed her eyes, like she was trying to fight off a headache. "Did you really sign up for the two-hundred-meter dash at Sectionals?"

Natalie shrugged defensively. "Yeah, so what?"

"You could have stuck with the four hundred and been happy with your success, but *no*, you had to poach the two hundred too. The two hundred is *my* event."

Natalie laughed harshly. "*Your* event? You don't own a whole event."

Maia folded her arms. "How would you have felt if I had competed in the four hundred? Before you were fast. I would have beat you every time, and you would have hated it."

"Guess what, I can compete in whatever event I choose to, and the best runner will win. It's not my fault you can't take a little competition. You just miss when I was slow—"

"I miss when you were still competing in field events!" Maia shouted. "I'm 'the Track One' and you're supposed to be 'the Field One.' It was so much simpler that way!"

Natalie spluttered angrily. "You're upset because I finally got good at something I love?"

"No," Maia said through gritted teeth. "I'm upset because ever since you started improving your times, you've been unbearable to be around. Everyone on the team is sick of your cocky attitude."

"Oh sure," Natalie sneered, "that's why they text me all the time and invite me to hang out. Makes perfect sense."

"Really? They've been texting you all week?"

Okay, so the texts chains and hangout invites that had seemed never-ending just a week ago had suddenly slowed down. Natalie had told herself it was just because everyone was focusing up for the end of the season. Had it really been because they found her annoying?

"I mean, I just thought—"

"Remember when you ran in that practice heat with Kristin last week? First you wouldn't stop teasing her about winning, then—as if that wasn't enough—you offered to teach her a few tricks?"

Natalie winced. She had thought it was funny at the time, but hearing it repeated made her cringe. "Yeah, but—"

"No one likes a sore winner. I'll let you in on a little secret.," Maia leaned in, narrowing her eyebrows. "Coach Yeung told the varsity team to make sure you felt welcome. They're only hanging out with you because I *begged* them to include you."

Natalie couldn't believe what she was hearing. Was that really true?

"It used to be fun hanging out with you at track meets," Maia continued. "Now, I'm not even looking forward to Sectionals. That's a first for me."

Natalie bristled. "You're just nervous because you know I'm going to beat you in every event." She stormed out of the room, fuming.

"May the best runner win!" Maia shouted after her and slammed the door.

10

Rather than feeling excited like she was expecting, Natalie found herself feeling nervous before the sectionals race. While her teammates around her were chatting before their races, Natalie stood quietly by herself. Maia was nearby, goofing off with the other varsity runners, but Natalie couldn't bear to approach them after her fight with Maia—especially now that she knew how they felt about her. She saw Jordan standing off with some of the other runners who weren't competing in the qualifying races but had still come to the meet to support the team. Jordan had been avoiding eye contact with her all day.

By the time the 400-meter dash was up next, Natalie's stomach was tight with knots. She shook out her hands and feet, trying to remind herself that this was what she'd been working so hard for. She couldn't step away now. She had earned this.

Natalie and seven other runners took their places in their numbered lanes. The starting blocks were arranged in a staggered formation along the curve of the track just behind the starting line. Natalie glanced at the other runners and to her surprise saw that her sister was a few lanes over.

What's Maia doing here? Natalie wondered. *Of course*, she realized with a sinking feeling. *I tried to horn in on the two hundred, so now she's here to steal the four hundred from me.*

She tried to catch her sister's eye, but Maia stared straight ahead with a look of grim determination and refused to look at her.

Natalie barely heard the announcer send them off, and before she knew it she was sprinting down her lane. She kept her speed in check but still raced past the other runners.

She came in first place, nearly five seconds faster than the next runner. Maia came in third, but Natalie knew that was still impressive for someone who had just jumped into the event.

Their team cheered for both sisters as they walked away from the track, but several of the varsity runners gave Maia an extra pat on the back and congratulations.

Natalie felt a pang of jealousy surge through her. She was the one who'd worked so hard and improved so much over the past few months. Why were they giving Maia so much attention?

She took that anger and frustration to the track for the 200-meter dash. Once again, she and Maia were in the same heat. Natalie made a point of not looking at her sister this time.

The runners took off, and Natalie was surprised at how quickly the 200 went by compared to the 400. Before she knew it, she had already crossed the finish line. She and Maia had been close, but Natalie had given herself a little jump in the last few seconds and pushed through first once again.

She couldn't help but jump in the air after she finished—she'd actually beaten Maia at her own event. Maia stared at her, jaw dropped. Natalie expected their teammates to congratulate her, but most of them kept their distance, watching both girls in awkward silence.

Natalie felt her stomach drop. She opened her mouth to say something, but Maia clenched her jaw and stormed past without giving her a second glance.

When Natalie found their grandparents later on, she was surprised to hear that Maia had taken a ride home with Kristin instead. She reminded herself that she'd qualified for not only one but two races at State. And even though she'd beaten Maia, her sister still qualified. Natalie should have been thrilled, but instead all she felt was guilt.

***

On the drive to State, Natalie stared out the car window at the passing scenery without really seeing it. Her grandma and grandpa chatted in the front seats of the car.

Maia had insisted on driving separately. Usually they carpooled to track meets. She hadn't made a big deal of it, since she didn't want their grandparents to know they were fighting, but Natalie bet that they knew anyway. They had been guardians to Maia and Natalie for too long to be fooled by forced politeness and stiff smiles. But they hadn't let on that they noticed. Natalie figured they were hoping she and her sister would figure things out and make up on their own.

Natalie felt queasy. She always felt nervous before races, but usually Maia was in the backseat with her, sharing gossip she had heard about the track stars from other high schools and chatting excitedly. But now Natalie was alone with her thoughts in a stuffy car.

She rolled down the window a crack, enjoying the feeling of fresh air on her face. She put in her headphones, intending to listen to music to make herself feel better. Then she realized with a sinking feeling in the pit of her stomach that they were already slowing down and turning into the parking lot of where the competition was being hosted. For the first time since she had woken up with superpowers, Natalie wasn't looking forward to running.

After her school's team was checked in, then they met as a group for stretches, warm ups, and pep talks. Then they dispersed to wait for their events. Natalie wandered around by herself again. Her grandparents had found seats in the stands with the other family members and spectators. Jordan wasn't responding to any of her texts and seemed to be actively avoiding her. Natalie watched Maia talk with Kristin and Jimmy and pretended not to notice the way Maia's smile didn't seem as genuine as it usually was.

Natalie felt a hollowness gnawing at her insides. Was it guilt? Shame? Embarrassment? Anxiety? *Probably all four at once*, she thought, grimacing to herself. How had she managed to alienate both her best friend *and* her sister in such a short time? And it was obvious that Coach Yeung thought she was too arrogant, now that Natalie thought back to the conversation they had had. Even her grandparents probably thought she had been too proud. She realized now why the other team members were so supportive of Maia. No matter how well she did, how many races she won, she was always a good sport and a good teammate.

Lost in this fog of dark thoughts and anxiety, Natalie still wasn't feeling ready when it was time for the 400-meter dash. She briefly considered not racing at all, but she told herself that would be silly. She had worked so long and so hard to get to this point, and she had hurt so many people. If she backed out now, all of her personal sacrifices—and all of the friendships she now realized that she had sabotaged— would be for nothing.

Once again, Natalie spotted her sister a few lanes over as the runners came to their starting blocks. After the announcer started them off, she was surprised to realize she wasn't even enjoying herself while she ran around the track. This used to be what she lived for, but now, Natalie found herself questioning why she was even doing this.

She didn't have more time to think on it. Before she knew it, she was crossing the finish line. She'd come in first place. Her teammates and Coach Yeung cheered for her and she could see her grandparents waving their arms in the stands, but Natalie barely even heard the roar of the crowd. It didn't even feel like a win at this point.

11

Natalie was dreading the 200-meter dash. When the announcer called "Runners to your marks!" she watched Maia step to her starting block. Then she sighed and told herself to focus. She quickly got into position.

Soon, this whole stupid affair would be over, and Natalie could take her shiny first-place State trophies home and hide in her room until everyone stopped being mad at her.

"Set!"

Natalie could feel the intense focus of every runner on the track as they set their sights on the race ahead of them.

"Go!" the announcer shouted, accompanied by the blast of the starting gun.

Natalie knew as soon as she started running that her start had been nearly flawless this time. It was comforting to know that there was still something she could practice to improve at, and that her efforts really did make a difference regardless of her superpower.

She sped around the track, outpacing almost everyone in the first few seconds.

Almost everyone, she realized, as she caught sight of her sister out of the corner of her eye, racing along right on her heels.

Natalie knew that she could accelerate to supernatural speeds and end this race in the blink of an eye, but where would be the challenge in that? She wanted to *earn* that trophy.

Neck and neck, Natalie and Maia zoomed around the first curve. And then, as they headed down the straightaway toward the finish, things seemed to slow down.

Natalie could see the finish line ahead of her. She had never even dreamed about winning the 200-meter dash at State, and now it was right there. All she had to do was reach out and claim it.

But her sister was beside her. Maia, who had wanted to be a track star for even longer than Natalie. Maia, who had been there for Natalie every night after their parents died, when she woke sobbing from nightmares. Maia, who had supported Natalie's switch from shot put to running and had applauded Natalie's efforts every step of the way, even though Maia wasn't used to having to share the spotlight.

Maia, who'd nicknamed her the Queen of the 400. The 200 was Maia's event.

So close now. The finish line was only a few strides away, even as each step, each breath, seemed to stretch out into an eternity.

Was it really worth being fast—finally being good at something she loved—if it meant jeopardizing the happiness of the *people* she loved?

And in that instant, Natalie knew what she had to do.

As the finish line loomed ahead of her, jolting her focus back to the present, Natalie slowed down ever so slightly, struggling against the momentum that threatened to carry her forward. No one else would be able to notice the last-minute change in her speed, but she hoped it would be enough.

The runners surged forward, and Natalie crossed the finish line a split second behind her sister.

The times were so close that the judges had to review video footage of the finish line. It was officially announced that Maia had finished first and Natalie finished second. Natalie sighed in relief and realized she had been holding her breath.

"Hey," she said, calling Maia's attention. "Nice race. Seriously. And . . . I'm sorry for being such a jerk these past few weeks."

For a moment Maia simply stared at her. Natalie gave a nervous smile. Then Maia wrapped her up in a crushing hug, nearly crying with happiness, her anger forgotten for the moment at least.

Natalie hugged her back fiercely, laughing.

In the commotion of the crowd, Natalie saw some of the other runners pointing excitedly at her and Maia.

"Those two are *so* crazy fast," she heard one say. "Can you believe they're sisters?"

"That's one talented family," the other runner responded.

Natalie felt like she was glowing. She would never have imagined she would be so happy to come in second.

***

As Natalie walked with Maia and their grandparents to their cars, she caught sight of Jordan across the parking lot.

She jogged over to her, trying to blurt out an apology before Jordan could even say anything.

But her friend was smiling. "Good race, Nat."

"Thanks. Oh man, Jordan, I am so sorry—"

Jordan held up a hand to cut her off. "I know you're sorry. And I also know that you let Maia win the two hundred. There's no way anyone could beat you unless you let them." She gave Natalie a proud smile. "You did the right thing in the end. Of course, I totally knew you were going to make the right decision the whole time—"

"Oh, hush," Natalie laughed. "Maia deserved that win anyway. Even if I wasn't going at top speed, I'm still surprised she managed to keep up with me."

Jordan gasped. "What if your sister has superpowers too?" she whispered excitedly.

Natalie laughed, but the suggestion tickled a thought in the back of her mind.

It would make sense, she thought. *Maybe running really is in our genes.*

She turned her attention back to Jordan. "Wanna hang out after school on Monday?"

"Can we do something besides training?" Jordan smirked.

"I insist that whatever we do has absolutely nothing to do with track."

"How about a movie?" Jordan suggested.

"That sounds perfect," Natalie said.

***

Their grandparents took them out to dinner to celebrate that their granddaughters were two of the fastest sprinters in the entire state. Their grandma, at Natalie's insistence, took a picture of the two of them with their first-place trophies to use in her article.

As they left the restaurant, Maia pulled Natalie aside. This time though, she wasn't angry.

"So, are you all right with me being the fastest in the school for a little while longer?" Maia asked with a smirk.

"Sure, you won that race fair and square," Natalie said.

Maia laughed. Natalie couldn't tell if she believed her.

"After you graduate, though," she told Maia, "I'm totally coming for all your records!"

"That's fine," Maia said, "because I'll be at college, setting new records for you to come break in two years."

College track, Natalie mused. *Working together on a relay team, we'd be unstoppable . . .*

They linked arms and turned to catch up with their grandparents.

"One thing I still don't understand, though," Maia said. "How *did* you improve so much, so quickly? And don't you dare say it was protein and water."

"Actually," Natalie leaned in and spoke quietly, "I have the craziest story to tell you . . ."

THREE MONTHS LATER

TRACK SUPERSTARS OUTRUN TRAGEDY

Last weekend, local track star sisters saved the life of their grandfather. While on a camping trip with his wife and granddaughters, Mr. Santos suffered an unexpected heart attack. With no cell service to call an ambulance, Natalie Santos ran for help, while her sister, Maia Santos, performed CPR until the ambulance arrived. It should be noted that the nearest town was twenty miles away. Maia Santos was unable to help clear up this confusing aspect of the story, saying that she has "no idea" how her sister made it there so quickly. But more important, Mr. Santos is expected to make a full recovery.

HAVING A SUPERPOWER IS NOT AS EASY
AS THE COMIC BOOKS MAKE IT SEEM.

CHECK OUT ALL OF THE TITLES IN THE

SUPER HUMAN

SERIES

MIND OVER MATTER

NOW YOU SEE ME

PICKING UP SPEED

STRETCHED TOO THIN

STRONGHOLD

TAKE TO THE SKIES

ABOUT THE AUTHOR

Raelyn Drake lives in Minneapolis, Minnesota, with her husband and rescue corgi mix, Sheriff, who can easily outrun both of them.